forever friends

Sofia's Puppy Love

American Girl®

forever friends

Sofia's Puppy Love

By Crystal Velasquez

SCHOLASTIC INC.

Special thanks to Dr. Heather Wiedrick for her veterinary expertise.

Published by Scholastic Inc., *Publishers since 1920.* SCHOLASTIC and associated logos are trademarks and/or registered trademarks of Scholastic Inc. The publisher does not have any control over and does not assume any responsibility for author or third-party websites or their content.

Book design by Yaffa Jaskoll

ISBN 978-1-338-11497-3

10 9 8 7 6 5 4 3 2 18 19 20 21 22

Printed in the U.S.A. 23

First printing 2018

To the hardworking people at animal shelters and rescue organizations everywhere.

–C.V.

Table of Contents

Chapter 1: Hide-and-Seek

Sofia Davis marveled at the nest of cat hair at the bottom of the cage as she pulled on a pair of bright yellow gloves.

"Wow . . . I had no idea cats shed so much," she said, wrinkling her nose. "Yuck!"

Sofia's friends Keiko Hayashi, Madison Rosen, and Jasmine Arroyo squeezed in next to her and peered into the cage. It was a Saturday, and, as usual, the four friends were volunteering

at Rosa's Refuge Animal Shelter along with Jasmine's veterinarian mother, Dr. Arroyo.

"Sorry, Nugget," Sofia added as she glanced down at the orange tabby. "No offense."

"Come on, fur ball," Madison cooed as she scooped up the cat. "Let's get you settled in an empty cat carrier while we clean your cage."

Jasmine grinned at Sofia. "If you think a little cat hair is gross, how are you going to own a dog? Most dogs shed even more than cats. And you'll have to pick up poop on walks at least twice a day."

"True!" added Keiko, nodding slowly. "I'm crazy about Sadie, but I'd love it if she learned to use a toilet."

Madison giggled. "That's why I have cats—they use a litter box!"

Sofia wished she could chime in with a pet story of her own. She wanted a dog more than anything, but her parents weren't eager to add a furry member to their family. For now, Sofia had to be content spending time with the dogs at the shelter.

"You know, comparing how much a dog sheds with how much a cat sheds would be a great science fair project!" Jasmine said. "Too bad I already decided to use a potato to make an electric circuit."

"I'm going to melt chocolate to figure out the exact temperature when it changes from a solid to a liquid," Madison said as she gently scratched Nugget behind her ears. "I'm going to see if melting different kinds of chocolate makes a difference."

"Yum!" Keiko replied as she held open a trash bag for Jasmine. "Afterward, you can eat all the chocolate!"

"Why didn't I think of that?" Jasmine said, sighing.

"Those are both great ideas," Keiko said. "I'm going to build a parachute for an egg. Hopefully I can drop the egg without breaking it! What about you, Sofia? Are you going to enter the science fair?"

"Yeah, you're the best science student in class," Jasmine added.

"I want to," Sofia replied. She twisted one of her reddish-brown braids around her finger thoughtfully. "I haven't come up with any great ideas yet. I'm just waiting to be inspire—"

Sofia was interrupted by two animal control officers hurrying through the door carrying a large dog crate. They were followed by Mrs. Wallace, the owner of the shelter.

"You can put her right here," Mrs. Wallace said, and the officers carefully set the crate down on the counter.

"We just need you to fill out these forms." The female officer held out a clipboard for Mrs. Wallace.

Sofia was dying to know what was going on. She glanced at her friends, but they looked just as clueless as she was. The girls waited patiently as Mrs. Wallace finished the paperwork. By the time the animal control officers had left, Sofia was ready to burst.

"Who's in the crate?" she asked Mrs. Wallace.

“This is a new resident,” Mrs. Wallace explained. “There were some reports that a dog had been abandoned in Greenlake Park. Those two officers responded to the call, and they found Penny and brought her here.”

The girls inched closer. Penny sniffed Jasmine’s fingers and wagged her tail. Then she lowered her snout onto her paws. She seemed friendly but tired.

“How do you know her name?” Jasmine asked.

“We don’t,” Mrs. Wallace explained. “But the officers named her on the way over here. It makes it easier to fill out the paperwork.”

She lifted the crate and carried it into the examination room.

"Come on, girls," she called over her shoulder. "It's time for her medical exam. She seems very gentle, so it's fine for you to watch."

Jasmine's mom gently removed Penny from the crate, and the girls gathered around the metal exam table. Penny lay there, tiredly resting her head against Sofia's hand. In this position, Sofia could see that the dog's stomach looked puffy.

"Is she sick?" Sofia asked with concern.

"I don't think so, but let's find out," Dr. Arroyo replied. First she examined the dog's eyes and ears. Then she took Penny's temperature.

"Her temperature is a little low," Dr. Arroyo said as she used her stethoscope to listen to the dog's chest.

"The heart and lungs sound good," she announced as she moved to Penny's stomach. She pressed the dog's belly gently, using her stethoscope to listen as well.

"Hmmm," Dr. Arroyo murmured. "That explains the low temperature."

"What is it?" Sofia asked, her face worried. "Is she okay?"

"She's just fine," Dr. Arroyo replied. "She's also pregnant. And by the looks of things, she's about two months along. She'll be giving birth any day now."

Madison stroked Penny's back and gave her a smile. "Hear that, girl? You're going to be a mom!"

"I'd like to do an X-ray so we can get an idea of how many puppies she's having," Dr. Arroyo told Mrs. Wallace. "The X-ray will also help me see how big the puppies are so I can determine whether Penny's likely to have any difficulties with the birth. Why don't you all wait in the other room and I'll call for you when I'm done."

Mrs. Wallace ushered the excited girls out of the exam room.

"Wow!" Sofia said. "We're going to have puppies! That's so exciting."

"*We*?" Jasmine teased her friend. "It seems like Penny's the one having the puppies."

"But the puppies will be born here at the shelter," Sofia replied, beaming. "And *we* all volunteer here. So yes, *we're* having puppies!"

A few minutes later, Dr. Arroyo poked her head out of the exam room.

"Okay, you can come in now," she said.

As soon as the girls and Mrs. Wallace were back in the room, Dr. Arroyo flipped a switch above the exam table. A screen lit up and an image appeared.

"Whoa!" Sofia cried, leaning closer. On the screen she could see the large curve of Penny's belly, and inside it what looked like a bunch of tiny skeletons. "Are those . . . skulls?"

"That's right," said Dr. Arroyo with a smile. "It's crowded in there, so I can't say for certain, but I think she's going to have five puppies." She pointed out each of the five skulls. She was about to turn off the screen when Sofia stopped her.

"Wait, isn't that another one?" she asked, pointing to a round object peeking out from beneath Penny's spine.

Dr. Arroyo peered closely at the screen. "Hmm . . . it's hard to say. It might just be some food in her stomach. Or you might be right. That could be a sixth puppy playing hide-and-seek."

Sofia grinned at what she hoped was one more puppy. "Found you!" she whispered.

Chapter 2: Runt of the Litter

It was Sunday morning and Sofia had just finished breakfast. She was clearing the table, but her mind was far, far away. She hadn't been able to stop thinking about Penny. How was she going to wait until her volunteer shift next weekend to find out how she was doing? Suddenly, Sofia had an idea.

"Mom? Dad?" she asked. "I don't have to be at soccer for a few hours. If we leave now, we could stop at the animal shelter on the way to my game to check on Penny. Pleeease?"

Mr. Davis put down the newspaper and checked his watch.

"It won't take long," Sofia said quickly. "I just can't stop thinking about her and wondering when the puppies will be born!"

"Okay," her mother said. "Rosa's Refuge *is* on the way to the field. Hurry up and get ready. But we won't be able to stay too long. You don't want to be late for your game."

"I know!" Sofia replied as she dashed upstairs to change into her uniform. "Thanks!"

Sofia and her parents arrived at the shelter half an hour later. Mrs. Wallace greeted them at the door, and Sofia was surprised to see Dr. Arroyo standing behind her in light green scrubs. The veterinarian usually only came on Saturdays. If she'd been called in, did that mean something bad had happened? Sofia hoped not!

"Hi, Mrs. Wallace, hi, Dr. Arroyo," Sofia said brightly. "We just stopped by to visit Penny on the way to my soccer game. I hope that's okay."

"Of course it is!" Mrs. Wallace smiled warmly. "In fact, you're just in time for a special surprise. Why don't you come see?"

Sofia and her parents followed Mrs. Wallace and Dr. Arroyo past rows of cats and dogs in their crates to a quiet area at the end of the hall where families spent time with dogs they were hoping to adopt. But today there was only one dog in the room: Penny. She was lying on a pile of soft towels, facing the wall. Sofia could hear soft squeaking noises that were too high-pitched to be coming from Penny. As Sofia came closer, she saw where the squeaking sounds were coming from. The puppies had arrived!

Sofia looked down at a row of hungry pups with pink noses and white, brown, and black fur latching onto their mother's belly to nurse. Their eyes were closed, and they were so tiny that Sofia could have held each puppy cupped in her hands.

"They were born just a few hours ago," Mrs. Wallace said.

Sofia beamed happily. "Nice to meet all one, two, three, four, five of you," she said, quickly counting the small, squirmy bodies. But then she frowned. "I guess I was wrong about there being a sixth puppy."

"Actually, you were right," Dr. Arroyo said. "Look there, at the very end."

Sofia followed Dr. Arroyo's finger to Penny's tail, where a very tiny puppy was snuggling into her fur.

"Look, Dad!" Sofia exclaimed. "That's the little hide-and-seek player I saw on the X-ray yesterday!"

"Your daughter has a very good eye," Dr. Arroyo told Mr. Davis. "We've named him Piper. The others are called Peaches, Poppy, Pickle, Peanut, and Princess."

"Phew!" Sofia exclaimed. "That sounds like a tongue twister!"

Everyone laughed.

"We hadn't thought of that," Mrs. Wallace admitted.

Dr. Arroyo pulled on a pair of gloves and scooped up the littlest pup. "Piper here is the runt of the litter," she explained. "They're all small, of course, but look at him. He's the tiniest."

"That's okay—small dogs are cute," Sofia said. "Besides, I used to be shorter than everyone else, but then I grew two whole inches over the summer. Now I'm one of the tallest girls in my class!"

"It's not that simple, Sofia," Dr. Arroyo replied gently. "Watch." She put Piper down right next to his siblings. The pup wiggled closer to his mother, but he was quickly pushed out by the bigger pups.

"See?" Mrs. Wallace added. "His size makes it hard for him to compete at mealtime."

"Runts can have a hard time," Dr. Arroyo explained, a serious look on her face. "We'll need to make sure he gets enough to eat and stays close to his family for extra warmth since he's so small. If he doesn't gain weight fast enough, he'll be vulnerable to infections and disease. Sometimes runts don't make it."

Sofia's eyes widened in surprise.

"You mean Piper might not live?" she whispered, her face pale. "Does he have a chance?"

Dr. Arroyo's face softened. "We'll do everything we can for him. If he puts on weight quickly, he should pull through."

Sofia's mother took her hand and squeezed, smiling encouragingly. Feeling more hopeful, Sofia smiled back. "So what can we do to help him?" she asked eagerly.

"First we'll keep their crate heated," Dr. Arroyo explained. "That way if Piper gets pushed away from his mother by his larger brothers and sisters, he won't get chilled."

"Piper will need to be bottle-fed, too, at least for a few weeks," Mrs. Wallace added.

"I'll help!" Sofia cried. "I bottle-fed the calves at Keiko's aunt's farm. I'd love to bottle-feed a puppy!"

"That would be great when you volunteer on Saturdays," Dr. Arroyo said. "But Piper has to eat every two to three hours. We'll need to

monitor how much he eats each day, along with his weight gain."

"Then I'll come to the shelter every day after school to help," Sofia said decisively.

Her mother cleared her throat. "Don't you have soccer practice two afternoons a week?" she asked. "And homework?"

"Oh yeah," said Sofia glumly.

Seeing her disappointment, her mother rested a hand on her shoulder. "Maybe we can compromise."

Sofia glanced up hopefully.

"You can come here two days during the week to look after Piper," Sofia's mother said, "but don't forget that school comes first."

"I know," Sofia said, nodding. "I'll keep up with all my homework; I promise!"

"Okay, then," Sofia's mother replied.

"Yes!" Sofia said, hugging her mom gratefully. Then she turned to Mrs. Wallace. "What can I do for Piper right now?"

"You can give him what every newborn needs: lots of love and attention," Mrs. Wallace replied.

Sofia grinned at the puppies. "That will be easy," she said.

Chapter 3: A Dream Come True

Two weeks later, Sofia joined her friends at the animal shelter. Just as they had the previous weeks, the four girls headed straight for the puppies. Now that they were a little older, they'd started to look like miniature versions of Penny—an adorable mix of beagle and hound, with floppy ears, big clumsy paws, and short stubby legs.

"Poppy is my favorite. She's so curious!" Jasmine said as she watched the pup investigating every corner of the litter's small pen.

"And Pickle is doing his favorite thing: eating!" Madison said.

Keiko laughed. "Is food all he thinks about?"

"My mom told me newborn puppies spend most of their time eating and sleeping for the first two weeks," Jasmine said.

"Pickle has the eating part down, that's for sure!" Keiko joked. She crouched in front of Peanut and Princess. "These two are so cute together!" she squealed.

Sofia was in love with all the puppies. But if she had to pick her favorite, she'd choose Piper. During every visit to the shelter, she had been charting his weight and temperature. At that moment, he was cradled in her arms, drinking lazily from a bottle of formula. She loved the little patch of white fur on his snout that was shaped like a heart.

"How's he doing?" Jasmine asked Sofia.

"He's a little behind in weight gain," Sofia explained. "Puppies should double their weight the first week. After that, they should gain 5 to 10 percent more each week. He eats, but he never quite finishes a bottle."

"Maybe that's because he keeps falling asleep during mealtime," Jasmine pointed out. Sofia looked down to find Piper's mouth still on the bottle, though his eyes were closed.

"Hey, you're not done yet," cooed Sofia, but it was no use. Piper was fast asleep. Sofia held up the bottle and saw that Piper had finished nearly half. "Not bad," she said. "That's more formula than he used to drink." She put the bottle down and reached for a small notepad on the table beside her.

"What's that?" asked Jasmine.

"We've been keeping track of how much he eats and how much weight he's gaining," Sofia explained.

Madison peered over Sofia's shoulder at the chart she had created. "Wow. You even wrote down how much all the other puppies weigh and their temperatures, too. I never would have thought to do that."

"Yeah, you've been busy!" Jasmine agreed.

Sofia looked down at Piper, now snoring adorably in her arms. Nothing else seemed to matter.

"I know," she replied, cuddling the tiny pup closer. "But Piper's worth it. He really needs me right now."

When her parents arrived an hour later to pick her up, Sofia brought her mom and dad over to Piper's crate right away to show off the puppy. He was sleeping beneath a heat lamp, his tiny paws twitching as he dreamed.

"Isn't he the cutest?" she asked softly.

"He *is* pretty adorable," her mom agreed, putting her arm around Sofia's shoulders.

"Sofia's doing a wonderful job with him," said Mrs. Wallace. "And I've needed all the help I can get! It will get even busier around here once I get the puppy webcam set up. We're hoping a livestream video of the puppies will drive up interest in adopting them."

Sofia felt a sudden ache in her heart. She wanted the puppies to find forever homes, of

course. Still, the thought of them leaving the shelter made her sad, too.

Sofia knew there was only one way to cure her heartache. She turned to her parents.

"Let's adopt Piper and take him home with us right now!" she blurted out. "I know what he needs and how to take care of him."

Her mom turned to face Sofia. She sighed. "Sweetheart, puppies are a lot of work, as you know. And we have a lot going on at home already. Your dad and I are remodeling the spare room, you have school and soccer, and your father and I are at work all day, so we wouldn't be home to walk and feed the puppy while you're at school."

"Your mother's right, sweetheart," her

father agreed. "I'm afraid this just isn't a good time to bring a puppy into our home."

Sofia swallowed the lump in her throat. She could see her dream of adopting Piper slipping away. "But I can take care of him; I promise! I know so much about dogs now. Just ask Jasmine!"

Jasmine, Keiko, and Madison had been silently watching from a few feet away. "It's true," Jasmine replied. "Sofia's the puppy expert of the four of us."

Her mother glanced at the puppy again, and then back to Sofia. "I know you've wanted a dog for a long time, Sofia," she admitted. "And you *have* been working hard—"

Mrs. Wallace cut in. "It's great that you're thinking about adopting, but none of the

puppies are ready for their forever homes just yet. They need to stay with their mother for at least eight weeks. They still have a ways to go."

"Right," Sofia mumbled. "I almost forgot."

Sofia's father glanced at her mother, who gave a subtle nod. He gently tugged on one of Sofia's braids. "Tell you what—if you show your mom and me that you can continue helping out here with Piper while keeping up with your homework and soccer practice, then as soon as Piper's old enough, he can come home with us."

Sofia gasped. "Really?"

"Yes, really," her dad answered, flashing a smile.

Sofia leaped up to grasp both of her parents in a tight hug. She was finally getting a dog of her own!

Chapter 4: A Change of Heart

On Monday, Sofia floated into school. On Sunday, her team had won their soccer game. And she hadn't been able to stop thinking about Piper all weekend. Finally, she would have a dog to take to the park or snuggle up with while she read books. She had already figured out where his bed would go. Sofia had never been this happy in her life.

She arrived early and slid into her desk. Then she unzipped her backpack and pulled out

her notebook and homework folder. But as soon as she saw the folder, her stomach sank.

"Oh no," Sofia groaned.

"What's wrong?" Keiko asked.

"I completely forgot to do my homework over the weekend!" Sofia whispered. Ms. Chen had given them math and writing assignments.

Sofia quickly took out her notebook and a pencil and started to write. By the time Ms. Chen took attendance, Sofia had finished one messy page for her writing assignment. She knew it wasn't great, and her math worksheet was still completely blank. But she hoped her teacher wouldn't notice.

Then Sofia glanced over and saw Madison pulling out her science fair registration form.

Sofia squirmed in her chair. She had forgotten that, too! Today was the deadline to register for the fair! She had been looking forward to it, too. Last year in second grade, her photosynthesis project had won a prize. Now she wouldn't be able to participate in the fair at all. Ms. Chen had been firm about the registration deadline.

Ms. Chen collected the homework assignments and the science fair forms, and then their school day began. The rest of the morning flew by, but Sofia no longer felt like she was on cloud nine.

When Ms. Chen dismissed the class for lunch, Sofia heard her teacher call her name.

"Sofia? I'd like to speak with you for a moment, please."

"Do you want us to wait for you?" Jasmine whispered.

Sofia shook her head. "That's okay. I'll see you in the cafeteria."

"Good luck," Keiko whispered. Madison gave her an encouraging smile. As Sofia walked back to Ms. Chen's desk, she had a sinking feeling she knew what her teacher was going to say.

Ms. Chen rifled through the stack of science fair registration forms.

"I had a chance to look through these, and I didn't see yours," Ms. Chen noted. "I know how much energy you devoted to your project last year, and I was wondering why you decided not to enter the fair this year."

Sofia sighed and slumped her shoulders. "I was planning to, but I forgot the form was due today," she explained sadly. "And I haven't come up with an idea yet anyway."

Ms. Chen nodded thoughtfully. "Does this have anything to do with your incomplete homework assignment?" she asked gently.

Sofia hung her head. "I'm sorry," she whispered. "I forgot to do that this weekend, too."

Ms. Chen looked at Sofia sympathetically. "Well, it happens to everyone from time to time," she said. "And there's always next year for the science fair. But make sure you turn in next week's homework on time."

"I will," Sofia said eagerly. "I promise!"

Sofia's teacher smiled. Sofia felt a little

better, but she knew she still had to talk to her parents about her homework and the science fair. Sofia hoped they would be as understanding as her teacher had been.

After school, Sofia's mom picked her up to drive her to Rosa's Refuge.

"Hi, sweetie," her mom greeted her warmly. "How was your day?"

"It was okay," Sofia said with a quick shrug as she slipped into the back seat of the car. Her stomach felt queasy. She really didn't want to tell her mom about her homework and the science fair project, but she knew she had to.

"Just okay?" her mom asked. "Did something happen?"

"Um, yeah," Sofia admitted slowly. "I forgot to do my homework this weekend. And I missed the deadline to register for the science fair."

"Oh, Sofia," her mom said. "You love the science fair! What happened?"

"I don't know," Sofia admitted. "I've been trying to come up with an idea, and I just haven't been able to. And this weekend I was so busy with Piper and soccer, I forgot all about it."

"Sweetheart, I know your dad and I said you could volunteer at the shelter during the week, but it sounds like you have a little too much on your plate right now," her mom said. "I think after today it would be best if you go back to volunteering on Saturdays only."

Sofia sat straight up in her seat. "But, Mom—"

"We had a deal," her mom cut in. "You already have soccer two days a week. And we agreed to let you volunteer at the shelter, too, but only if you kept up with your schoolwork. Remember?"

"Yes," Sofia mumbled. "I'm really sorry."

"I know you are," her mom said gently. "And given what happened, I'm not sure you're ready to own a dog yet, either." Sofia could see her mom's face in the rearview mirror, and she didn't look happy.

She gasped. "But what about Piper?"

"I'm sure Mrs. Wallace will find him a good home," her mother said sympathetically. "But a dog is a big responsibility, and it isn't a decision to take lightly. We'll get a dog when you're

ready for it. That's only fair to you, to us, and to the dog."

Sofia blinked back tears. Her heart felt as though it had been crushed into a thousand pieces. For the rest of the ride to the shelter, she could hardly breathe.

Chapter 5: Friendly Advice

After her mom dropped her off at Rosa's Refuge, Sofia rushed to see the dogs. Penny was in the grooming area with one of the adult volunteers, and her puppies were playfully wrestling in the pen. One little pup wagged his tail and let out squeaky barks as soon as he saw Sofia.

"He's been waiting for you," Mrs. Wallace said, her eyes twinkling as she handed Sofia a pair of gloves.

A lump had formed in Sofia's throat and tears welled in her eyes. But she blinked hard and tried her best to focus on what she was there to do. She gently lifted Piper out of the pen and placed him on the scale to measure his weight before his feeding. When she marked it on her chart, Sofia saw that he had gained a bit since her visit on Saturday. The supplements and the heat lamps and extra love were working! Sofia knew she should have been happy at that realization, but she couldn't shake her sadness.

Still, she had a job to do. She carefully measured and mixed a bottle of formula for Piper. Then she scooped him up and settled herself in a chair to feed him. When she held the puppy close to her chest, she could feel that he was a little heavier, and his eyes were bright and alert. He showered Sofia with doggy kisses and tried to climb onto her shoulder. That would usually thrill her, but today it only made her sad. Despite all her efforts, tears slid down her face as the puppy gulped down his bottle.

Mrs. Wallace noticed Sofia was upset, and she gently took Piper away and placed him back in the pen. Then she sat down next to Sofia.

"Want to tell me what's wrong?" she asked, handing Sofia a tissue.

When she could finally speak, Sofia found the words hard to say. "Mom and Dad decided not to adopt Piper after all."

Mrs. Wallace listened carefully as Sofia told her everything. When she had finished, Mrs. Wallace pulled her into a warm hug.

"I know you're upset," she said. "And I understand that it's terribly disappointing that your parents changed their minds. But even if you can't adopt a dog, there are plenty of other animals and people here at the shelter who need you each Saturday."

Sofia sniffled. Mrs. Wallace was right, of course. She didn't have to own a pet to help take care of one. But somehow it just wasn't the same.

The next Saturday was the first that Sofia had spent away from the shelter in a long time. Down the hall, her parents were noisily working on the spare room, moving everything out so they could paint. Meanwhile, Sofia was sprawled on her bed, reading. But she found it hard to concentrate. When the video chat on her computer chimed, she welcomed the interruption.

She opened her laptop, clicked a button, and Jasmine's face appeared. Behind her, cat posters lined the wall and puppies yipped in the background. Jasmine was in Mrs. Wallace's office.

"Hi," Sofia said, trying to sound happier than she felt.

"Hi, Sofia," Jasmine replied.

Madison squeezed into the frame on Jasmine's left. "Where are you?" she asked, a concerned look on her face. "We miss you!"

Suddenly, Keiko's face popped in from the right. "Yeah, is everything okay?"

Sofia gave her friends a sad smile. "Not really," she said. "I still can't believe I won't be

taking Piper home. To tell you the truth, I just couldn't bear to see him today."

Jasmine nodded understandingly. "I'm sorry you can't adopt Piper," she said. "He missed you today, too. It's not as fun when you're not here."

"Thanks," Sofia replied.

"We have some news," Jasmine said, taking a deep breath. "Penny and Pickle just got adopted."

Sofia shot to her feet as her heart leaped into her throat. "What? I don't believe you."

"See for yourself," Madison said. "Log in to the shelter's webcam."

Sofia had been so busy wallowing over Piper, she'd forgotten about the webcam. She clicked open a new window and typed in the web address. Soon a live video appeared on

the screen. Five puppies were in the pen, sleeping. But Penny and Pickle were gone.

"The two families who will be adopting Penny and Pickle are hanging out with them in the playroom," Keiko explained. "They won't take them home for a few more weeks, though."

"This is terrible!" Sofia cried sadly. "I mean, it's great that they found homes, but I didn't know it would start happening so soon. With the webcam bringing people in, all the puppies will get adopted in no time. And then I'll never see Piper again."

"You don't know that for sure," Keiko said softly.

"I really blew it," Sofia said. "My parents don't think I'd be a good dog owner now. Maybe they're right."

"That's not true," Madison said encouragingly. "You'd be great."

"Right!" Jasmine agreed. "Just find a way to prove that you're responsible enough. Then maybe your parents will change their minds about Piper."

"Do you really think so?" Sofia asked, wiping away a tear.

"It's worth a try," Keiko replied. "If anyone can do it, you can."

Chapter 6: One Big Mess

After she hung up, Sofia went to talk to her parents. Maybe if she asked, they would tell her what she could do to prove how responsible she could be. But when she entered the hallway, she found her parents coming out of the spare room. Her mom clutched her stomach, looking pale.

"Your mother's not feeling well," her father said.

Now that Sofia thought about it, her mom hadn't been feeling well for the past couple of days, especially in the morning.

"I'm taking her to lie down. Could you put the lid back on the paint can? I don't want the paint to dry out."

"Okay, Dad," Sofia replied. "Feel better, Mom." She watched them leave, and then peeked into the spare room. It was empty except for a few buckets of paint and a couple of brushes. Her parents had been working hard in there, but if her mom was sick, the painting would have to wait.

Unless I do it for them! Sofia thought suddenly. Not only would she be helping her parents, but she'd show them she could handle a big job by herself. This was the perfect chance to prove how responsible she was. She'd never painted a room before, but Keiko had painted sets for one of their school plays once and it looked fun. How hard could it be?

Instead of putting the lid on, Sofia dipped a brush into the can of light green paint and started to slather it on the wall. The first few brushstrokes looked great. *This will be easy!* she thought.

She continued to paint, covering half of one wall.

I've totally got this! Sofia thought confidently. She started to do a little victory dance to celebrate. But as she twirled across the room to dip her paintbrush again, she stumbled and kicked the pail over. Thick green liquid poured across the hardwood floor.

"Nooo!" Sofia whispered frantically. She righted the bucket, scooping up as much paint as she could, but a river of paint continued to ooze across the floor like foam-green lava. She

ran to the bathroom down the hall to grab a roll of paper towels. She was halfway back when she skidded to a halt and looked down in horror. She'd forgotten to put down the paintbrush before her mad dash to the bathroom! Now there were globs of paint splattered all along the hallway, and behind her was a trail of light green footprints.

She gasped and lifted up one foot. Paint coated the bottom of her sneaker. She must have stepped in one of the globs!

"Nice going, Sofia," she groaned to herself.

Deciding the mess in the hallway wasn't as bad as the one in the room, she hurried on to the first spill, unspooled a few paper towels, and tried to wipe up the paint. But instead of cleaning up the spill, all she managed to do was

spread it around. Even worse, bits of paper towel had ripped off and were stuck in the paint. Sofia stood up, staring at the damage in shock.

"What on earth?" a voice boomed.

Sofia whirled around to find her father standing in the doorway, his mouth hanging open. She looked around to see the room as he saw it. It seemed as though there was paint everywhere except on the walls.

"I—I'm helping?" Sofia stammered as she glanced up at her father. From the look on his face, she could tell he wanted to yell—or laugh—but he seemed too exhausted to do either. Instead he just sighed.

"Thanks for trying," he said. "But why don't you take off your sneakers and go clean yourself up? I'll take care of this."

Sofia carried her sneakers with her to the bathroom, careful not to touch any walls. She felt awful. She'd tried to be responsible and help out, but all she'd done was make things worse. After she'd scrubbed the paint off her hands and put her clothes in the sink to soak, she texted her friends the bad news.

Chapter 7: A Second Chance

The next morning, Sofia's doorbell rang bright and early. She knew her mom still wasn't feeling well, so she hurried to answer it. Through the glass panes on either side of the door, she saw her friends standing on her porch.

She opened the door and took in Jasmine's old jeans and blue bandanna. Her long corkscrew curls were pulled back into a ponytail. Keiko had on paint-splattered overalls, a striped T-shirt, and a rainbow-colored headband. And

Madison wore a red baseball cap with the brim to the back and a pair of gray sweatpants. An oversized cat T-shirt topped off the strange look.

"What's going on?" Sofia asked. "What are you doing here? And what's with the clothes?"

Keiko held up a bag full of smocks, paintbrushes, and cleaning supplies. "We're here to help you paint."

"Your text last night made it sound like you needed us," Jasmine said.

"Wow," Sofia said, surprised. "That's really nice of you, but I doubt my dad will let me help with the painting again," she said. "He spent last night cleaning up the floor, thanks to me. So I'd have to ask him if it's okay for you to help."

"They already did," said a voice behind her. She swung around and saw her father smiling

down at her. "They called early this morning to ask my permission. I decided the more help we have on that room, the better."

Sofia beamed at her friends, almost too grateful for words. "Then let's get started!"

She directed her friends to the spare room while she changed into an old pair of jeans and a T-shirt. When she returned, her dad was pouring paint into four plastic trays. He assigned each girl to paint a different part of the wall while he used a long roller to get the parts near the ceiling.

"Ready, set . . . go!" he said.

Together they started to paint. It was hard work, but it was also fun. Somehow they still got plenty of paint on themselves, but most of it ended up on the walls, where it belonged. In

just a few hours they were done, and the room looked beautiful.

"Excellent job, girls!" Sofia's father said, smiling. "Thank you for all your help. It would have taken me a lot longer to do this all by myself."

Sofia smiled at her friends. With their help, she'd fixed her painting mistake. But she knew it wasn't enough.

The next day at school, when Ms. Chen dismissed her class for lunch, Sofia didn't head to the cafeteria with her friends. Instead, she marched up to her teacher's desk.

Sofia felt nervous all of a sudden. Would she be able to do this? She glanced at the door where Jasmine, Madison, and Keiko were

watching her from the hallway, giving her smiles and thumbs-up to boost her confidence. Sofia turned back to Ms. Chen.

"I know I missed the deadline for the science fair," she began, "but if you'll let me, I'd really like to enter a project."

Ms. Chen leaned back in her chair. "I don't know," she said thoughtfully. "The other teachers and I already began planning the table arrangements in the gym. We want to be sure there's enough space for all the projects. Do you have something specific in mind?"

Sofia's shoulders slumped. "Not exactly," she admitted. "But I know I can come up with something quickly!"

Ms. Chen gazed at Sofia for a long time. "All right," she said. "I'd be happy to give you a

second chance. But you don't have much time! Here's a fresh form. Write up a plan for me over lunch period, and then I'll take a look. If it looks like a good project, I can squeeze you in as a late entry to the fair."

Sofia jumped to her feet. "Thanks so much, Ms. Chen!"

With that, she practically skipped out of the room, clutching the science fair form in her hands.

"Good for you!" Jasmine said, greeting her friend with a high five.

"Way to go," Keiko chimed in.

"So what now?" Madison asked as they walked toward the cafeteria.

Sofia looked determined. "Now I just have to come up with the best science fair project ever!"

Chapter 8: Furry Inspiration

As the girls settled in at a cafeteria table to eat lunch, Sofia placed the science fair project form next to her tuna sandwich. Meanwhile, Jasmine flipped through their science book as she crunched on some baby carrots. "How about making a volcano?" Jasmine suggested.

Sofia shook her head. "I tried making one over the summer and I added too much baking soda. There was fake lava everywhere. After that disaster with the paint, I think I'll steer clear."

Keiko's eyes lit up. "Ooh, how about a model of the solar system? I have some blue glitter you can use to make the Earth."

"Good idea," Sofia replied. "But I think Michael Abiola is already doing a solar system."

"Too bad," Keiko replied. "I'm dying to use that blue glitter on *some*thing!"

Jasmine flipped to another page in her book. "I don't see anything in here that'll work," she said. "All the good ones take time, like this one where you feed plants different liquid diets to see which one makes them grow fastest."

Madison pointed at the chart under the description of the plant experiment. "Hey, that kind of looks like the chart you made for Piper," she told Sofia.

Sofia gasped. "Madison, you're a genius!"

Madison lifted one eyebrow in confusion. "I am?"

"Yes!" Sofia cried. "Piper can be the subject of my science fair project!"

When Sofia got to the shelter that Saturday, she was extra excited. Not only would she get to see Piper, but she also had a great plan for her project. She told Mrs. Wallace all about it as soon as she arrived.

"I'll show everybody how to take care of runts so they get stronger and healthier, just like Piper," she explained.

"That sounds like a terrific idea." Mrs. Wallace beamed. "You've certainly worked wonders with Piper. He's dying to see you."

Sofia couldn't wait to see him, either. But when she entered the room with the puppy pen, she was shocked to see not just her friends but a roomful of visitors, all buzzing around the puppies.

"What's going on?" Sofia asked Madison.

"It's the webcam," her friend replied. "Now that the puppies are almost ready to be adopted, everybody wants to meet them in person."

Sofia watched as the puppies tumbled around their pen. It was almost as if they were putting on a show by being extra adorable. Peanut and Princess trotted around the pen, side by side, carrying two ends of the same chew toy in their mouths. Peaches was snuggled up next to Penny, and Poppy was sniffing all the new visitors like crazy. Pickle had his face buried in a bowl of dry dog food, his new favorite meal. Sofia noticed that Mrs. Wallace had placed matching ribbons around all the adopted dogs' necks that said I'VE BEEN ADOPTED! Penny and Pickle were wearing them, and Sofia saw a ribbon each on Peanut and Princess, too. It was great that the livestream had generated so much interest, but it worried Sofia, too. There were only three dogs left. What if someone adopted Piper?

Sofia looked around in a panic. Where was he, anyway? She couldn't see him. But then she spotted him, snuggled under a blanket, hiding from the crowd. As soon as he saw Sofia, he

wriggled out and bounded over, letting out excited yips.

Dr. Arroyo appeared next to Sofia, smiling down at Piper. "He's almost the same weight as his brothers and sisters now—thanks to you." Dr. Arroyo patted Sofia's shoulder. It was more great news, but Sofia couldn't enjoy it because of the conversations she was hearing around her.

"Pick out whichever one you want," said a dad to his son.

Sofia watched anxiously as the boy spent a few minutes playing with each puppy. *Please don't pick Piper,* she pleaded silently, holding her breath.

After a few long minutes, the boy stretched out his arm and pointed to Poppy. "That one!"

Sofia breathed a sigh of relief when she watched the father tell Mrs. Wallace the good news. As Mrs. Wallace placed an I'VE BEEN ADOPTED ribbon around Poppy's neck, Sofia knew it was only a matter of time before someone chose Piper.

Suddenly, Sofia had a great idea. When Mrs. Wallace had a free moment, Sofia approached her. "I think I know how to make my science fair project extra special," she told Mrs. Wallace, "but I'll need your help."

Chapter 9: The Science Fair

Two weeks later, everyone in school gathered in the gymnasium for the annual science fair. It seemed like the whole town was there, with teachers and families strolling from exhibit to exhibit, admiring the students' projects.

Jasmine had managed to make a great electric circuit using a potato. She impressed the teachers by using it to turn on a small lamp. Madison set up a fondue pot to melt different kinds of chocolate bars. Beside her, Keiko had set up a ladder. She planned to drop her egg from the top in a special cushioned parachute she had designed and built herself. Next to the ladder was a poster with photos of all the times she had failed and broken the egg.

Sofia's presentation about runts had gathered quite a crowd. It showed all the charts Sofia had made tracking Piper's diet and weight for his first six weeks of life. But what really drew people over was the puppy movie Sofia had set up on her laptop. Mrs. Wallace had let Sofia record some of the video from the shelter's webcam, and Madison had contributed footage she'd taken with her phone showing Sofia patiently bottle-feeding and weighing Piper. Any time a group passed Sofia's table, they oohed and aahhed at the adorable puppies.

Sofia was pleased, but she couldn't help feeling anxious about Piper. He and Peaches were the only puppies left. It was just a matter of time before some lucky person adopted them, too. In her mind, she tried to be okay with that. She knew that the important thing was that Piper found his forever home, even if it wasn't with her.

"You should be very proud of your daughter, Mr. Davis," Ms. Chen was telling Sofia's father. Her mother wasn't feeling well again, so she had stayed home.

"Thank you," he replied. "And thanks for offering her a second chance at the science fair."

"Actually, she's the one who came to me," Ms. Chen admitted, smiling at Sofia. "I wasn't sure she could pull it together in time, but she

proved me wrong. Nice work, Sofia. This is real science: collecting data, making careful observations, and reporting on it so that others can learn what you've learned."

Sofia grinned at the compliment. "Thanks, Ms. Chen," she said.

Sofia's father took another long look at her project. The video showed Piper diving under the blankets, then popping his head out and panting happily. Piper was playing hide-and-seek just as he'd done before he was born. "You know," her father said to Sofia, "he really is pretty cute. What do you say we go adopt him after the science fair is over?"

Sofia thought she'd heard him wrong. "Are you serious?" she asked. "But what about everything you said before about me not being

responsible? What about the mess I made with the paint?"

Her father laughed. "That *was* a mess," he admitted, "but you helped me clean it up. And the fact that you asked your teacher for a second chance shows maturity. I can see how hard you worked with Piper. I think your mother would agree with me that you've proven how responsible you can be. You'll be a great dog owner."

Sofia couldn't believe it.

"Jasmine! Madison! Keiko!" she shouted to her friends from across the gym. They had been studying Madison's project—and sneaking tastes of chocolate—but they hurried over right away.

"You guys—my dad said I could adopt Piper!" she practically shouted. The four friends started jumping up and down and screaming with excitement.

"Girls!" Sofia's dad interrupted the celebration, his hands over his ears. "I think you'd better quiet down. You don't want to break those test tubes and cause an explosion."

He gestured toward the project next to Sofia's, which contained beakers full of different-colored liquids.

"Sorry, Dad," Sofia said sheepishly. "We're just *so* excited!"

"Well then, what are we waiting for?" her dad said. "Let's head over to Rosa's Refuge right away."

Sofia said good-bye to her friends and promised them an update as soon as she got home.

When Sofia and her dad got to the shelter, Mrs. Wallace met them in the reception area. "Sofia!" she exclaimed. "I was just about to give you a call. I have some news—"

"So do I," Sofia interrupted excitedly. "I'm here to adopt Piper! My parents changed their minds!"

Mrs. Wallace's face fell. All the light in her eyes seemed to dim. "Oh, Sofia . . . that's why I was going to call. A family came in this morning. They have twin daughters, and they decided to adopt a puppy for each girl."

Sofia shook her head. "You don't mean . . ."

"They adopted Peaches . . . and Piper," Mrs. Wallace confirmed sadly. "Since the puppies are weaned now, they took them home an hour ago. I'm so sorry."

Sofia was speechless. Although the shelter was filled with the noise of barking dogs and meowing cats, Sofia could almost hear her heart crack like one of Keiko's eggs.

By the time Sofia and her dad got home, there was no consoling her. "I never even got to say good-bye," she wailed when she saw her mother. Tears streamed down her face as she crawled into bed next to her mom, who wrapped her in a tight hug.

"I'm so sorry, sweetheart," her mom said. "I know how much you cared about Piper. But there will be other dogs you'll love, too."

"Not like Piper," Sofia insisted.

Her mother shared a look with her father. "There might be one thing that will cheer you up. Should we tell her?"

Her father shrugged. "Seems like as good a time as any."

"Tell me what?" Sofia asked, sniffling.

Her mother reached into her dresser and pulled out something that looked a lot like the X-ray Dr. Arroyo had taken of Penny. Except this one was dark and swirly, and instead of six tiny skulls, Sofia saw one round head with a tiny five-fingered fist right next to it.

"You're going to be a big sister, Sofia," her mom explained. "I'm having a baby."

"You are?" Sofia asked in shock. "Really?"

"Yes, really," her dad replied. "We hope you're as excited about the news as we are, but we understand that it's a lot to take in."

Sofia couldn't believe it. She had always

wanted a baby brother or sister, but she just figured she was destined to be an only child.

"I'm excited," Sofia replied, a smile spreading across her face. "I'm just surprised. Why didn't you tell me? Is it a boy or a girl? And is that why you've been sick in the morning?"

"Whoa, whoa, whoa," her mom replied with a laugh. "One question at a time!"

"Sorry," Sofia said sheepishly. "I just really am excited. And surprised. Wow! I'm going to be a big sister!"

Her mom nodded. "You are, sweetheart," she replied. "I'm sorry we didn't tell you sooner, but we didn't want to get your hopes up in case something went wrong. The beginning of a pregnancy can be pretty rough. The babies don't always make it. But I'm feeling better now, and the baby is doing really well."

Her mother lay her hand protectively over her belly. Sofia thought about Piper and how he almost hadn't made it.

"Do you know if it's a boy or a girl?" Sofia asked again, holding up the sonogram.

"Not yet," her father replied. "We want it to be a surprise. But whatever the baby is, we'll love it."

Sofia smiled. She was still sad about Piper, but she was thrilled at her parents' surprising news. Soon she would have a little brother or sister!

Suddenly, she gasped and sat straight up in the bed. "The spare room—it's for the baby!"

"That's right," her mother replied. "And

now that you know who the room is for, you know that we have to make it extra special. We could use a responsible person like you to help us. What do you say?"

Sofia cozied up to her mom, putting her hand over her mother's hand. "I'm in!" Sofia cried.

For a moment, the crack in her heart hurt a little bit less.

Chapter 10: Surprise Delivery

Sofia tilted her head to one side and then the other. “Mmm, I think it would look better over there,” she said. She pointed to the rocking chair next to the new crib.

Madison picked up the soft yellow pillow. “But that’s where we had it in the first place!”

“Sofia, I think you’re overthinking this,” Jasmine said gently. “You’ve had the pillow in

four different places, and it looked good in all of them."

Keiko chuckled. "Her poor dad had to move the crib five times!"

Sofia blushed and gave her friends a sheepish grin. "I just want this nursery to be perfect."

"It already is!" Jasmine insisted, sweeping her arm around the room.

Sofia stood back and tried to see it through her friends' eyes. Her mom and dad had moved all the big furniture pieces in—the crib and dresser, the rocking chair, the changing table—and now Sofia was in charge of decorating. She'd taken the job very seriously, trying to find just the right spot for all the adorable baby things. There was an owl-shaped lamp on the dresser, and stuffed bears lined the crib. The soft blankets in the crib and the foam-green walls made the room feel warm and cozy. She'd hoped it would get her mind off Piper, but she still thought about the tiny pup all the time.

"It does look pretty great," Sofia said at last. "I think we're done."

"Hooray!" her friends cheered.

Sofia went to get her parents, making them close their eyes until they stood in the middle of the room. It had been two months since they'd revealed their big news, and Sofia's mom was wearing a loose blue summer dress that showed her growing belly.

"Are you ready?" Sofia asked them.

"Ready!" her parents answered in unison.

The girls counted off together: "One, two, three . . . open your eyes!"

Sofia's parents slowly opened their eyes and burst into huge grins. "Oh, Sofia, it's wonderful!" her mom gushed.

"It's perfect," her father cheered. "Great job, sweetheart!"

"My friends helped," she said, smiling gratefully at them.

"Hey, we should get over to the shelter," Keiko reminded them. "Mrs. Wallace said she needed our help with a dog that just came in."

Mrs. Wallace was waiting for them outside the shelter, and she seemed nervous. But when she saw Sofia and the girls approaching, she smiled. "Thank you for bringing them on a Sunday," she said to Sofia's parents. "I'm sure you had lots of things to do, but this simply couldn't wait."

"It's no trouble," Sofia's mother assured her.

"Is everything okay?" Sofia asked, worried.

"Well, I pride myself on finding the right forever home for each animal," Mrs. Wallace replied. "But every now and then, a family realizes they made a mistake, and they bring the adopted animal back. That's what happened this morning. The dog is here now and he looks lost. I can't even get him to eat any treats."

"That's terrible!" Jasmine cried.

"If anyone can cheer him up, it's you four." Mrs. Wallace opened the front door and motioned for them to follow her inside as she led them to the playroom.

Sofia looked around, but all she saw was a lumpy blanket in the corner.

"Where's the dog?" she asked Mrs. Wallace, confused.

At the sound of Sofia's voice, the lump under the blanket began to squeal and wriggle. A second later, one stubby paw and a snout with a small patch of white fur shaped like a heart poked out eagerly.

"Piper?" Sofia gasped in disbelief.

Piper lifted his head and yipped happily. He leaped to his paws, throwing off the blanket and running to Sofia at top speed. She bent just in time to scoop Piper up into her arms. "Hi, boy!" she called out. "I missed you!"

"He missed you, too," said Madison. "Look how excited he is. But why did the family bring him back?"

Mrs. Wallace shook her head. "Two puppies were too much for them to handle. And Piper never seemed happy there. So they brought him back, hoping I could find him a better fit."

"Looks like you've found one already," said Sofia's mother with a laugh.

Sofia felt hope spark inside her like fireworks. "Can we really keep him?"

Her parents both gave her glowing smiles.

"Absolutely," her father said. "Piper is coming home with us today!"

Sofia grinned as Piper nuzzled his wet nose against her neck.

"Your forever home is with me now," Sofia told him as she kissed his fuzzy head.

About the Author

CRYSTAL VELASQUEZ was born in the Bronx, New York. She studied English and creative writing at Pennsylvania State University and is a graduate of NYU's Summer Publishing Institute. She lives in Flushing, New York, and hopes to adopt a new puppy very soon.